TAFT MIDDLE SCHOOL MEDIA CTR
30007000171768 741.5 LOV
Groot #3

W9-CMZ-856

DATE DUE			

GUARDIANS OF THE GALAXY
GROOT #3

MARVEL
marvelkids.com
© MARVEL

ABDO
Spotlight

ABDOPUBLISHING.COM

Reinforced library bound edition published in 2018 by Spotlight,
a division of ABDO, PO Box 398166, Minneapolis, Minnesota 55439.
Spotlight produces high-quality reinforced library bound editions for
schools and libraries. Published by agreement with Marvel Characters, Inc.

Printed in the United States of America, North Mankato, Minnesota.
042017
092017

PUBLISHER'S CATALOGING IN PUBLICATION DATA

Names: Loveness, Jeff, author. | Kesinger, Brian ; Gandini, Vero, illustrators.
Title: Groot / writer: Jeff Loveness ; art: Brian Kesinger ; Vero Gandini.
Description: Reinforced library bound edition. | Minneapolis, Minnesota : Spotlight, 2018. | Series: Guardians of the galaxy : Groot | Volumes 1, 2, 4, and 6 written by Jeff Loveness ; illustrated by Brian Kesinger. | Volumes 3 and 5 written by Jeff Loveness ; illustrated by Brian Kesinger & Vero Gandini.
Summary: When Rocket and Groot are on an intergalactic road trip, the two get separated and it's up to Groot to help his friend. Whatever comes this famous talking-tree-thing's way, one thing's for sure… it's going to be a Groot adventure!
Identifiers: LCCN 2017931596 | ISBN 9781532140778 (#1) | ISBN 9781532140785 (#2) | ISBN 9781532140792 (#3) | ISBN 9781532140808 (#4) | ISBN 9781532140815 (#5) | ISBN 9781532140822 (#6)
Subjects: LCSH: Superheroes--Juvenile fiction. | Adventure and adventurers--Juvenile fiction. | Comic books, strips, etc.--Juvenile fiction. | Graphic novels--Juvenile fiction.
Classification: DDC 741.5--dc23
LC record available at https://lccn.loc.gov/2017931596

Spotlight

A Division of ABDO
abdopublishing.com

GROOT, EVERYONE'S FAVORITE TALKING TREE THING, WAS HOPING TO TAKE AN INTERGALACTIC ROADTRIP TO EARTH WITH HIS BEST PAL AND FELLOW GUARDIAN OF THE GALAXY, ROCKET RACCOON.

A DANGEROUS BOUNTY HUNTER NAMED *ERIS* DERAILED THEIR PLANS, THOUGH, HOPING TO CLAIM A BOUNTY ON GROOT'S HEAD! SHE HAD TO SETTLE FOR CAPTURING ROCKET, AND IS NOW USING HIM AS BAIT TO LURE GROOT OUT INTO THE OPEN.

GROOT'S HOT ON THEIR TRAIL, BUT HAS CROSSED PATHS WITH A PAIR OF FRIENDLY FACES – THE SILVER SURFER AND DAWN GREENWOOD!

JEFF LOVENESS
WRITER

BRIAN KESINGER
ARTIST

VERO GANDINI
COLOR ARTIST

JEFF ECKLEBERRY
LETTERER

DECLAN SHALVEY & JORDIE BELLAIRE
COVER ARTISTS

DEVIN LEWIS
EDITOR

SANA AMANAT
SUPERVISING EDITOR

NICK LOWE
SENIOR EDITOR

AXEL ALONSO
EDITOR IN CHIEF

JOE QUESADA
CHIEF CREATIVE OFFICER

DAN BUCKLEY
PUBLISHER

ALAN FINE
EXEC PRODUCER

GROOT CREATED BY STAN LEE, LARRY LIEBER AND JACK KIRBY

OW...
WELL, USUALLY THIS IS WHERE WE EXCHANGE INSURANCE INFORMATION.
SORRY... WE'VE MET, RIGHT? I'M MEETING A LOT OF NEW PEOPLE THESE DAYS...
I AM GROOT.
HI, GROOT. I'M DAWN GREEN-WOOD.
I AM GROOT.
OH NO... DID WE... IS HE OKAY?
HE IS GROOT. THAT IS WHAT HE SAYS.

PTTZZ
PTTZZ
I AM GROOT
I DON'T THINK HE'S OKAY...

WE HAVE SAVED MANY IN THE PAST, MY FRIEND...
...BUT NOW I SEE YOU HERE, LOST IN THE SPACEWAYS... ALONE.
AND I KNOW YOU.

IT IS A LONELY EXISTENCE... TO HAVE SO MUCH INSIDE, BUT NO MEANS TO EXPRESS IT...
TO BE IMPRISONED WITHIN YOURSELF.

I KNOW THIS PRISON BETTER THAN MOST.
FOR OUT HERE IN THIS UNTOUCHED SEA OF STARS, WITH NOTHING BUT THE POWER COSMIC TO GUIDE ME, STAND I, THE SILVER SURF--
STOP.

STOP WHAT?
STOP SURFERIZING.
SURFERIZING?
WE DON'T HAVE TIME FOR ONE OF YOUR 40-MINUTE SPACE SOLILOQUIES.
YOU DO THOSE. A LOT.

HE NEEDS HELP. SO LET'S HELP HIM.

SEEMS LIKE YOU WERE LOOKING FOR SOMETHING... OR SOMEONE.
KNOW WHICH WAY THEY WENT?
I AM GROOT.
OUT THERE?
HOW 'BOUT IT, NORRIN? CAN WE DO "OUT THERE"?
YES. WE CAN.

"HERE?
"HOW ABOUT HERE?
"PROBABLY NOT HERE..."
ARE YOU SURE THAT TRACKING THING EVEN *WORKS?*

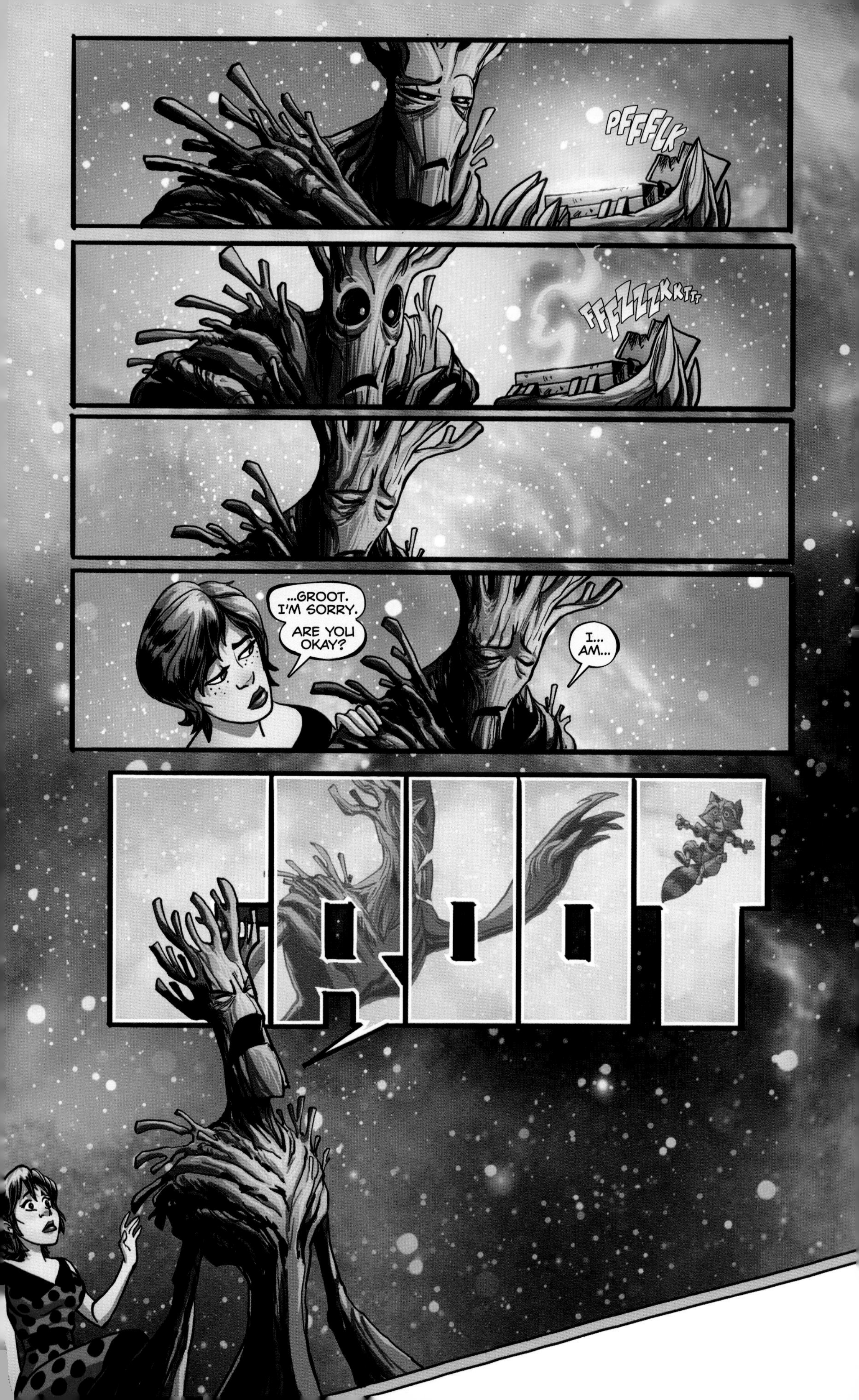
PFFFLK
FFFZZZKKTTT
...GROOT. I'M SORRY.
ARE YOU OKAY?
I... AM...
GROOT

TALK TO HIM.
WHAT?
YOU'RE BOTH... Y'KNOW... SUPER HERO SPACE GUYS.
IF YOU'RE GOING TO SURFERIZE, NOW'S THE TIME TO DO IT.

TALK TO HIM.
TOOMIE AND I ARE GONNA GO LOOK AT THAT WEIRD MOON THING.
DON'T FORGET TO KEEP LETTING ME BREATHE IN SPACE. THAT'D BE BAD.

AHEM
I DO NOT KNOW WHAT HAS HAPPENED OR WHAT YOU HAVE LOST...

...BUT IF I WAS TO GUESS, IT WOULD BE A FRIEND.

THE COSMOS... CAN BE AN EMPTY PLACE WITHOUT SOME-ONE TO SHARE IT WITH. I KNOW THIS.

"I BECAME THE HERALD OF GALACTUS TO SAVE MY WORLD... BUT IN THE PROCESS, DOOMED SO MANY.
"I SOARED THE SPACEWAYS... ALONE WITH MY CRIMES... MY GUILT.
"I WAS SO VERY LOST...
"I DID NOT BELIEVE I DESERVED REDEMPTION.
"OR HAPPINESS...

"BUT THEN I MET PEOPLE WHO SHOOK ME FROM MY APATHY.
"I MADE FRIENDS.
"I FOUND MYSELF AGAIN."

AND NOW, SHE IS HERE WITH ME...
STRANGE... HOW ONE PERSON CAN MAKE LIFE FEEL SO NEW.

I TELL YOU ALL THIS TO SAY I KNOW THE VALUE OF MAKING FRIENDS. AND I KNOW THE GRIEF OF LOSING THEM... OF FAILING TO SAVE THEM.
YOU DROWN YOURSELF IN BLAME... BUT PLEASE KNOW THIS:
YOU ARE STILL HERE.

I HAVE DONE TERRIBLE THINGS I SHALL NEVER ATONE FOR.
BUT I AM HERE. TODAY.
AND TODAY, I CAN STILL CHOOSE TO DO GOOD.
SO I WILL.
UH... NORRIN.

IS THAT BAD? IT LOOKS BAD.

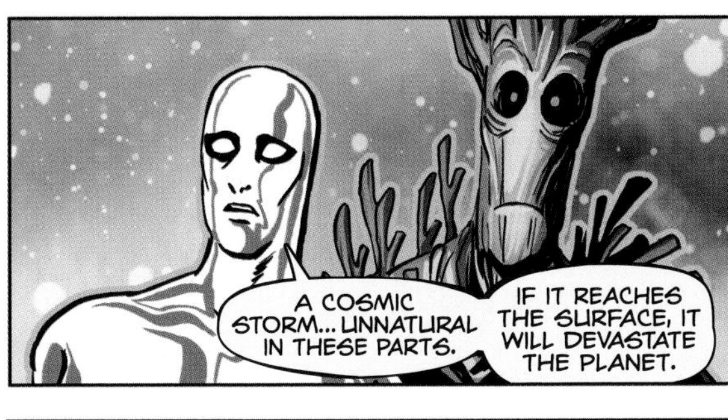
A COSMIC STORM... UNNATURAL IN THESE PARTS.
IF IT REACHES THE SURFACE, IT WILL DEVASTATE THE PLANET.

SHALL WE DO GOOD?

I AM GROOT.

I'M GONNA CALL THAT A YES...

SKOOOOMMMMM!

BRAKOOMM

GET THE PEOPLE TO SAFETY...

EVERYONE, GET INSIDE! TAKE COVER!
...DO YOU SPEAK ENGLISH? OR DO I JUST SOUND LIKE A CRAZY PERSON?
...*I* SHALL DEAL WITH THE STORM.

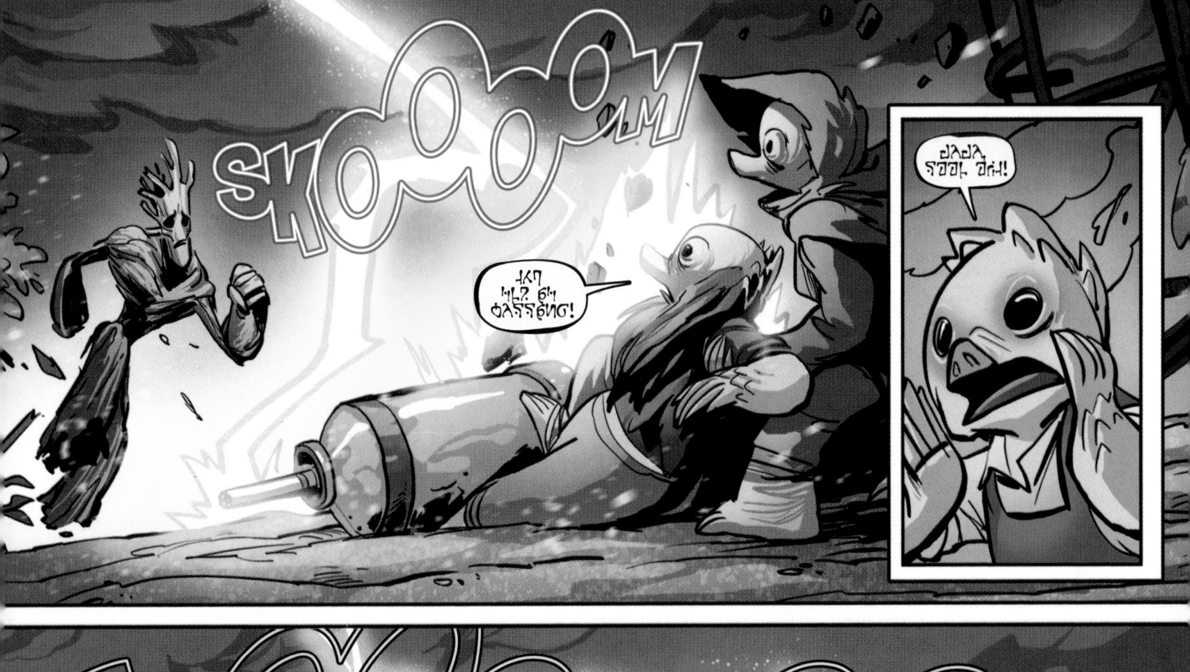
SKOOOOM

SKOOOOOOOOOM

I AM GROOT.

GROOT! THESE PEOPLE DON'T HAVE SHELTER!

WOW. WELL, THAT SOLVES THAT. YOU OKAY, PAL?
I AM... GROOT.
GOOD TO KNOW.

I AM GROOT?!
OH, DON'T WORRY ABOUT NORRIN...

"...I THINK HE'S GOT THIS."
BRAAAAAM!
I AM GROOT.
YEAH...

...HE HAS HIS MOMENTS.

IS EVERYONE SAFE?
YEAH. GROOT HERE TOOK A HIT FOR THE TEAM, BUT HE SAVED A LOT OF PEOPLE...

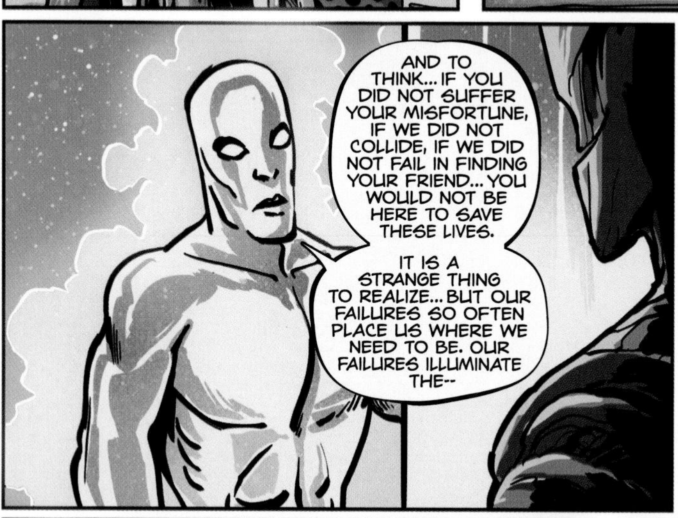
AND TO THINK... IF YOU DID NOT SUFFER YOUR MISFORTUNE, IF WE DID NOT COLLIDE, IF WE DID NOT FAIL IN FINDING YOUR FRIEND... YOU WOULD NOT BE HERE TO SAVE THESE LIVES.
IT IS A STRANGE THING TO REALIZE... BUT OUR FAILURES SO OFTEN PLACE US WHERE WE NEED TO BE. OUR FAILURES ILLUMINATE THE--

ILLUMINATE THE...
NORRIN?

...WHAT WAS I SAYING?

I WAS HOPING TO LURE SOMEONE POWERFUL WITH THAT LITTLE SHOW... BUT I NEVER IMAGINED I'D TRAP SOMEONE SO POWERFUL.
NORRIN, WHAT'S WRONG?!
AAARRGH!

AND NOW I FEAST UPON THE POWER COSMIC!
WHAT IS THAT THING?
DAWN, GET OUT OF HERE!
GO!
FRAAADOWWW!
I'VE ALREADY HAD A TASTE, SURFER.
ZZZUURM
NOW ACARI MUST HAVE IT ALL.
NYULLLGH!!

KRAKKOOOOOMMM

BBTTTZZZ
THOOOOOOMMM

HSSSSSSS
GLLLLH!

OH, THANKS. AIR'S COOL. I MISSED AIR.

ANYONE HUNGRY?
I AM GROOT.
SOUNDS GOOD.

HERE.
WHAT IS THIS?
IT'S A BLANKET. WHEN SOMEONE'S SICK, WE WRAP 'EM IN ONE.
I REQUIRE NO BLANKET.
WELL, REQUIRE ONE ANYWAYS. YOU'VE HAD A BIG DAY.

THANK YOU, DAWN...
FOR EVERYTHING.
I AM... STRUGGLING TO FIND WORDS...
THAT'S A FIRST.

IT IS...

I AM GROOT!
YUP... NOBODY ELSE IS.
POP A SQUAT, GROOT.
THAT MEANS "SIT DOWN"... DUNNO KNOW HOW FAR EARTH-SLANG TRAVELS.

MY FRIEND, WITHOUT YOUR AID, NEITHER ONE OF US WOULD BE ALIVE TODAY...
FOR CENTURIES, I SOARED THESE SPACEWAYS ALONE. I HAD GROWN ACCUSTOMED TO THE ABSENCE OF AFFECTION...
BUT HERE, AT THE END OF THE UNIVERSE, I SEE THAT NOTHING IS MORE IMPORTANT THAN THE FRIENDS ONE MAKES ALONG THE WAY...
AAAAND YOU'RE BACK TO SURFERIZING ALREADY.
MUST BE FEELING BETTER.

FOR THE COSMOS... IS... A COSMIC... CELESTIAL... PORTENT... OF...
OF...
I'M SURE YOU WERE GOING SOMEWHERE WITH THAT...
COSMIC...
YUP.

I THINK ALL THAT MEANT "THANK YOU."
AND HE'S RIGHT. IT'S WEIRD TO THINK ABOUT...
...NONE OF THIS WOULD'VE HAPPENED IF WE DIDN'T RUN INTO YOU.

...IF YOU DIDN'T LOSE YOUR FRIEND... IF WE DIDN'T GET LOST, NORRIN WOULDN'T BE HERE TO SAVE THE PLANET. YOU WOULDN'T BE HERE TO SAVE THOSE PEOPLE. TO SAVE ALL OF US.
SOMETIMES OUR MISTAKES PUT US EXACTLY WHERE WE NEED TO BE...
I GUESS THAT'S WHAT I'VE LEARNED TO LOVE ABOUT TRAVEL...
YOU MEET SO MANY RANDOM PEOPLE. YOU'RE NOT SO CLOSED OFF. YOU'RE MORE OPEN TO YOURSELF...

EVERY-THING'S NEW AGAIN.
I DON'T KNOW A BETTER WAY TO BE.

I AM GROOT.

BLOOOMP
ROCKET RACCOON
450.100 876.43 KM

DON'T WORRY... TOOMIE AND I'LL TAKE CARE OF HIM.
I... LIKE SPACE...
I KNOW YOU DO, NORRIN.

HOPE YOU FIND WHAT YOU'RE LOOKING FOR.
IF YOU'RE EVER IN MASSACHUSETTS, LEMME KNOW. I CAN RECOMMEND A GREAT BED 'N' BREAKFAST.

NOW GET BACK OUT THERE.
TO BE CONTINUED!

GROOT

COLLECT THEM ALL!

Set of 6 Hardcover Books ISBN: 978-1-5321-4076-1

Hardcover Book ISBN 978-1-5321-4077-8

Hardcover Book ISBN 978-1-5321-4078-5

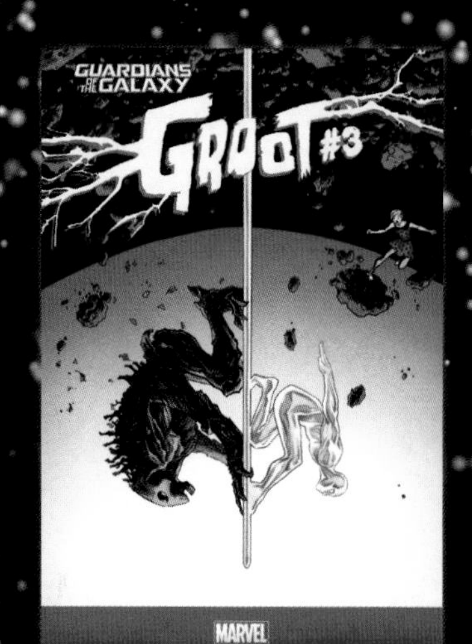

Hardcover Book ISBN 978-1-5321-4079-2

Hardcover Book ISBN 978-1-5321-4080-8

Hardcover Book ISBN 978-1-5321-4081-5

Hardcover Book ISBN 978-1-5321-4082-2